SECRET BEAST CLUB

THE UNICORNS OF SILVER STREET

SECRET BEAST CLUB

THE UNICORNS OF SILVER STREET

ROBIN BIRCH

ILLUSTRATED BY
JOBE ANDERSON

PUFFIN

With special thanks to Rachael Davis

PUFFIN BOOKS

UK | USA | Canada | Ireland | Australia
India | New Zealand | South Africa

Puffin Books is part of the Penguin Random House group of companies
whose addresses can be found at global.penguinrandomhouse.com.

www.penguin.co.uk   www.puffin.co.uk   www.ladybird.co.uk

First published 2023

001

Text copyright © Storymix Limited, 2023
Illustrations copyright © Jobe Anderson, 2023
The moral right of the author and illustrator has been asserted

Set in Dante MT Pro
Text design by Anita Mangan
Printed in Great Britain by Clays Ltd, Elcograf S.p.A.

The authorized representative in the EEA is Penguin Random House Ireland,
Morrison Chambers, 32 Nassau Street, Dublin D02 YH68

A CIP catalogue record for this book is available from the British Library

ISBN: 978-0-241-57348-8

All correspondence to:
Puffin Books, Penguin Random House Children's
One Embassy Gardens, 8 Viaduct Gardens, London SW11 7BW

MIX
Paper from
responsible sources
FSC® C018179
www.fsc.org

Penguin Random House is committed to a
sustainable future for our business, our readers
and our planet. This book is made from Forest
Stewardship Council® certified paper.

For Alice, my childhood bestie –

thank you for all the adventures!

PROLOGUE

Stop! Before you read this book, you must take the Secret Beast Club Oath:

I solemnly swear to protect magical creatures at all costs.

Do you swear?

(I can see if you've crossed your fingers behind your back – I am a ghost.)

Let me introduce myself: I am Pablo Fanque, the founder of the Secret Beast Club. For centuries, my descendants and I have guarded magical creatures that live in secret Bewilder Bubbles. Maybe there's a Bewilder Bubble near you right now. Bewilder Bubbles are rare and can only be seen by those with magic sight, and for good reason. Living within them are some of the most precious creatures in existence. That's right – I'm talking about dragons, phoenixes and even . . . unicorns!

What are *these Bewilder Bubbles?* I hear you ask. Well, you'll have to come along with my latest recruits to find out for yourself. In short, they were created in ancient times. Mystical creatures gifted certain humans with magic sight, and together they made the Bewilder Bubbles, intending to shield those within a bubble from people from the outside world who seek to harm them. They used the same rare magic to form living gargoyles too. You'll soon meet one: my oldest and dearest friend, Guy Goyle. He is helping my brave great-great-granddaughter Leila to continue my work. She needs all the help she can get now that time is against her. Magic sight fades with age and, between you and me, Leila isn't getting any younger!

·.·+·+·⁺·₊·⁺·.

Over time, fewer and fewer humans are born with this magic running through their veins. But there are still other humans who seek to hunt magical creatures. They belong to a dastardly organization called the Seekers of Unusual and Unique Creatures Society, or SUUCS for short.

But that's enough for now. Let's head to London – I sense a Bewilder Bubble disturbance in Hackney . . .

1
AISHA

Aisha couldn't believe her eyes. It had to be fake, surely?

'Jayden, you have got to see this!' she cried, pointing at her tablet.

'Hmmm?' Jayden's gaze did not leave his book.

'Seriously, you're going to want to watch this. It's about a unicorn!'

'Really?' Jayden said, finally looking up. He went over to her and squeezed on to the edge of Aisha's armchair. 'I was just reading about those. Here,' he said, shoving his book in front of her screen.

With a loud, exaggerated sigh, Aisha glanced at the page. She did a double take. It was a picture of the strangest creature she had ever seen. It had the body of a horse with the feet of an elephant and a really sharp-looking horn on the front of its head.

'What *is* that?' she asked.

'It's a monoceros.'

'A mono-what?'

'A monoceros,' Jayden said, grinning. 'It's related to the unicorn and according to *Beastly*

Adventures with Ancient Mythical Creatures –'

'Forget the bore-o-ceros,' Aisha said, and pursed her lips. 'Check out this video! You won't believe it but –'

'. . . the hairdresser didn't hear her right . . . Bright green, her hair was! . . . She put the pictures on her social media . . . Did you hear about . . .'

Aisha had been interrupted again! This time by loud laughter and familiar voices coming from the kitchen.

The Mums were gossiping, as usual. Aisha and Jayden's mums had grown up on the same estate and had been inseparable since they were little, so Aisha and Jayden had always been close, even though they couldn't be more different. They didn't really hang out at school – Jayden preferred reading in the library, while Aisha could usually be found in the playground learning the latest dance craze and joking around. Outside school, though, they hung out all the time, and Aisha couldn't imagine her life without Jayden in it. She knew they would be friends forever.

The laughter faded into hushed whispers, and Aisha groaned inwardly, exchanging a worried look with Jayden. The only time their mums went quiet like this was when they were plotting something.

'What a lovely day!' said Jayden's mum, bursting into the living room. 'All that sun and vitamin D.'

'You mean, all those car fumes polluting the atmosphere and dog poo on the pavement,' said Jayden.

'You two should go outside,' Aisha's mum said, ignoring Jayden completely. 'Get some *fresh* air.' Her gold hoop earrings bobbed enthusiastically as she nodded with encouragement.

The summer holidays had started just a week

ago and, ever since then, the Mums had been nagging Aisha and Jayden to go outside. Aisha really didn't understand why they were so keen to get them out of the house. She glanced at Jayden and could see that he was about to launch into his full list of 'One hundred reasons NOT to go outside', so to speed things up Aisha quickly interjected: **'Nothing interesting ever happens outside – EVER!'**

'Well, that's definitely not true,' said Jayden's mum, peering out of the window. 'Look what's coming up the canal.'

'What a peculiar narrowboat . . .' said Aisha's mum, joining her at the window.

Aisha slowly turned in her chair to follow their gaze. Their flat looked out on to the canal, and usually the narrowboats that moored outside all had the same boring design: deep blue or green, with white borders, which made them look like floating picture frames. But this new one *was* different and . . . well, strange-looking. Its side had been painted with a scene of a thick forest of trees; Aisha could make out unicorns playing in

THE NARROW ESCAPE

The Secret Beast Club

Guardians of Wild Magic

fallen leaves, and some kind of winged beast nesting in the branches.

'The *Narrow Escape* . . . Funny name for a narrowboat,' Aisha said.

'Oh, I think I read about this in the *Gazette*,' said Jayden's mum, tucking one of her long braids behind her ear. 'Apparently, it's a new narrowboat bookshop.'

'*Cooool*,' Jayden whispered under his breath, and pushed past the Mums for a better look. 'What does it say underneath the name? There are some words in gold, but I can't read them properly.'

'I can't see anything,' said his mum.

Aisha joined them at the window. 'It says: *The Secret Beast Club*.'

'Oh, yes,' said Jayden. '*The Secret Beast Club: Guardians of Wild Magic*.'

'Guess it's time for me to get those glasses,'

Jayden's mum said, frowning. 'I can't see it.'

'Me neither,' said Aisha's mum, squinting at where Jayden was pointing.

It was clear that Aisha and Jayden could see something their mums could not. *Strange*.

'The Secret Beast Club doesn't sound much like a bookshop,' said Jayden disappointedly.

'Perhaps it's one of those floating classrooms,' his mum replied.

'Floating classrooms?' Aisha's mum sounded far too curious for Aisha's liking.

'Yes! Cousin Chris went on one when we were kids. He couldn't stop raving about it. If this is something similar, you two would love it,' said Jayden's mum. 'They encourage kids to be nature explorers. You know, discover stuff about animals and plants as you travel along the waterways.'

'What a fabulous idea, eh, Aisha? Maybe you should go and check it out,' said her mum.

Aisha rolled her eyes. 'Sounds like school but in your spare time. No thanks.'

'Rubbish!' said her mum, folding her arms. 'It's nothing like school. It's about *exploring* in *nature*.'

'Ugh, nature is overrated,' Aisha said. Why on earth would she ever want to leave the comfort of her own cosy flat, to risk the unpredictable British weather, when she could do much cooler stuff *indoors*? Her mum had given Aisha her old tablet a couple of weeks ago, and Aisha had been glued to it ever since. She loved it so much that she wasn't bothered if she never went outside again. As long as she had enough battery and strong Wi-Fi, she had all she needed.

But Jayden was still looking at the narrowboat and Aisha could tell he was intrigued. She needed to step in before things got out of hand.

'Maybe we should go and –' he began.

Aisha grabbed Jayden and headed for her room.

'Don't fall for it, Jayden,' said Aisha. 'It's not a floating library – it's a school.'

Aisha pulled Jayden into her room. She knew that neither of them were into nature, and the idea of a classroom on a boat did NOT appeal, so it was best to steer clear of the Mums for a bit.

Aisha flipped the sign on her bedroom door from

to

Jayden settled down on the beanbag by the end of Aisha's bed and opened up his book again. The beanbag was actually Jayden's, brought from his home and left at Aisha's for times like this. He had his own makeshift bookcase too, made from an old fruit crate they'd picked up at the Saturday market.

Aisha sat on the edge of her bed. 'Now can I finally show you this video on my tablet? You won't believe it!'

'I'll look at it later,' said Jayden, already lost in his book again.

Aisha huffed and jumped up, putting her tablet on the windowsill next to her little cactus plant. She stared at Jayden with her hands on her hips. 'Jayden, seriously – get your head out of that book and let me show you this video!'

When Jayden ignored her again, Aisha walked over and yanked *Beastly Adventures* from his hands.

'Hey! Give that back!' Jayden cried, trying to grab it.

'No! I've had enough of your books.'

'Don't pull it! It'll rip!'

Suddenly, from over Aisha's shoulder, there came a loud **CRASH!** She whirled round to see her cactus on the floor, its pot broken in half. Out of the corner of her eye, she caught a glimpse of a grey blur leaping from her open bedroom window.

A *squirrel?* Aisha sighed. They were worse than pigeons, thinking they owned the place.

Then her eyes fell on the *empty* windowsill. Her heartbeat raced in her ears. 'Wait! Where's my tablet?'

'I don't know. It was there a second ago,' said Jayden.

'**Oh no! Did the squirrel knock it over the edge?!**' Aisha dropped the book and leaned out of the window, praying her tablet had landed in the soft shrubs below and not on the hard canal towpath. 'I can't see it!' she cried.

'Don't lean so far,' said Jayden, sounding nervous. 'You could fall!'

'We're on the first floor, Jayden,' Aisha said. 'And –' She broke off as she spotted the grey blur again. '**Look**, there's the squirrel! I bet it's got my tablet!'

The grey blur was fast . . . It seemed too big to

be a squirrel and Aisha wasn't exactly sure how a squirrel would carry a tablet . . . but, whatever the thing was, it looked like it was heading for the *Narrow Escape*.

'We *have* to get my tablet back,' she said to Jayden. 'What if that *thing* drops it in the canal? Mum would flip! I *promised* her I could be responsible. She'd never let me have another one and I can kiss goodbye to *ever* being allowed a phone!'

'It would serve you right for taking my book,' Jayden said, shrugging his shoulders and sitting back down on his beanbag.

'Oh, no you don't! Get up. You're coming too!' Aisha huffed, pulling on her trainers.

'No way,' said Jayden, crossing his arms.

'You *have* to come,' Aisha insisted. 'You're faster than me.'

'I didn't even *see* the squirrel take your tablet. It

probably just fell on the ground and, you know, smashed into tiny pieces.'

'*Something* took my tablet! Imagine if it had taken your book. Besides, you can't stay here by yourself. You'll have no one to help you fend off the Mums.'

Jayden huffed and put on his baseball cap, before reaching for his own trainers.

'We're going out,' Aisha shouted as they ran out of her room.

'**Out?**' called the Mums in unison from the kitchen. '**As in *outside*?**'

'Yeah, to get some fresh air, like you said, and maybe look at the new narrowboat.'

'Ooh, take a few close-up shots on Aisha's tablet. I want to see those gold letters you were talking about,' called Jayden's mum.

'Er . . . sure,' said Aisha, her stomach churning.

It was obvious that Jayden didn't really want to

come, but Aisha knew he would always have her back – that's what best friends were for. She just hoped that whatever had taken her tablet was going to return it.

2

JAYDEN

Jayden didn't know what was more unbelievable:

- ☺ Some kind of giant grey squirrel had snatched Aisha's tablet.

- ☀ The two of them were ACTUALLY going outside.

'Careful!' said Jayden as Aisha charged down the stairs two at a time.

By the time Jayden got outside, Aisha was already way ahead, running down the narrow canal towpath. Jayden groaned and broke into a jog to catch up with her. *Typical Aisha, always running into situations without thinking.* Jayden tutted to himself. *Typical me,* he thought, *obediently following Aisha to keep her out of any* real *trouble.*

'I'm pretty sure I saw that grey thing jump on to the *Narrow Escape*!' called Aisha.

'Are you sure?'

She nodded, chewing the end of one of her braids anxiously. Jayden's stomach dropped. If it was *anyone* else, he would not have set foot outside. But it was Aisha: his oldest and bestest friend since before they were old enough to talk. He couldn't let her down now.

'All right,' he said with a sigh. 'Let's check out the boat.'

Jayden shoved his hands into his pockets and cautiously walked towards the narrowboat. The *Narrow Escape* looked a lot shabbier up close. The paint was flaking off, and there was a big dent in the side of the boat by the front deck, next to something that looked strangely like a scorch mark.

Aisha stepped on to the deck.

'Hey! I didn't mean you should actually get **on** the boat!' Jayden shout-whispered.

'Keep watch, OK?'

'What if someone's in there?' Jayden hissed.

He closed his eyes and tried to think of happy things: his books, a nice warm sofa, fluffy slippers. He opened his eyes and his stomach filled with butterflies at the thought of what they were doing. Being outside in the first place was bad enough, but Jayden couldn't believe Aisha was trespassing on someone's *actual* private property.

'Don't sweat it,' Aisha said. 'The boat looks empty, and I'll be quiet.'

'How can I *not* sweat it?' Jayden said. His heart was drumming a fierce beat inside his chest.

Aisha sighed and rolled her eyes. 'If you're going to worry, then worry about the fact that the Mums can literally see what we're doing if they look out of the living-room window.'

Jayden hadn't even *thought* of that. That needed to be at the very top of his 'Reasons not to trespass on a narrowboat' list.

'This is *exactly* why going outside is *always* a bad idea,' he said, rubbing his brow.

'Keep your cap on,' replied Aisha. 'I'll be quick.'

There was no stopping Aisha once she'd made up her mind to do something, so he just watched on anxiously as she began to rummage through the tatty stuff on the front deck. She cast aside broken fishing rods, peered inside an old biscuit tin full of nails and different-sized nuts and bolts, and then dug out a boot with no sole.

Jayden's mind kept darting from one potential disaster to the next. What if someone walked past? What if the Mums really did look out of the window? What if someone else was on the boat?

'What's this?' said Aisha, interrupting his thoughts.

Jayden gasped. 'What *is* that?'

In Aisha's hand was a rope. But not a worn, slightly fraying, semi-damp kind of rope that you'd expect to find on an old narrowboat. This was a thick, silvery rope, shimmering in the sunlight, as if it was . . . magic. Aisha was pulling it out of an unremarkable-looking grey metal chest that was rusted at the corners. The strange thing was that the more Aisha pulled at the rope, the more it glowed.

BBBBRRRRRRRIIIIINGG!

A shrill ringtone made Aisha and Jayden jump.

SOMEONE WAS ON THE NARROWBOAT.

A lilting but impatient voice came from inside the cabin. 'I've found the permit, so you can stop with all that griping! Bye-bye now, Janice. And do use some apple cider on that ingrown toenail.'

'Aisha, we need to go n–'

The door burst open. Aisha dropped the rope. Jayden's heart sank. They were busted.

A tall woman stood in the doorway. Her deep brown skin glowed in the bright sunlight. She was wearing a black-and-white chequered top, trousers and a brightly patterned headscarf that reminded Jayden of the phoenix feathers he'd seen in his book on magical creatures.

'Who are you?' the

woman demanded, her eyes narrowing. 'And what are you doing on my boat?'

'H-h-her – um – t-tablet,' stuttered Jayden.

'A giant grey . . . squirrel thing . . . took it and ran over here, I think. Have you . . . seen it?' Aisha asked hopefully.

'You think that a "giant grey squirrel thing" stole your tablet and brought it on to my boat?'

'Well, now you say it back to me, it does sound a bit far-fetched,' said Aisha.

'On the contrary.' The woman grinned and then shouted behind her into the boat. 'Guy, come out! I can't believe our luck – we have a couple of kids here who can see you!'

Jayden and Aisha shared a puzzled look.

Get off the boat, Jayden mouthed.

Aisha edged towards him.

The woman tutted. 'Guy Goyle, come on! They're waiting!'

They heard a *thump, thump, thump* coming from inside the narrowboat. Then some*thing* appeared at the door. It was partly hidden in the shadows, but Jayden could just about make out a small, roundish shape that was no taller than the woman's knee.

The figure was muttering in a deep, gritty voice. Jayden could only hear snippets: 'not a squirrel . . . I resent the comparison . . . wasn't stealing – I was testing them . . .'

'Speak up, Guy!' exclaimed the woman. 'How many times do I need to remind you?'

'I said I was right! These kids *DO* have magic sight. Shame it looks as though they waste all their time indoors looking at screens.'

Aisha gasped. 'EXCUSE ME? How long I spend "looking at screens" is literally *none* of your business.' She kissed her teeth. 'And I'm not taking lectures from a thief!'

Jayden ignored Aisha and leaned forward, trying to get a better look at the creature on the boat. At this point he felt sure about three things:

☺ This thing called Guy had taken Aisha's tablet on purpose.

💡 Guy was not a giant grey squirrel at all.

🤖 Whatever Guy was, he was NOT HUMAN!

Jayden's palms were suddenly sweaty. He should be at home. It was *safe* at home. He needed to grab Aisha and get out of here. Jayden stepped on to the deck to pull Aisha back.

'The timing of this discovery could not be better!' The woman clapped her hands in delight.

'My ability to sense magic seers is impeccable,' Guy said, and sniffed. 'Here, have your contraption back!' A little grey hand emerged from the shadows and lobbed Aisha's tablet into the air.

Aisha caught the tablet, hugging it to her chest.

Jayden gasped. Guy's hand looked all crackly and hard. 'Is he made of *STONE*?' he cried.

'**Shush!**' The woman put a finger to her lips. '**Keep your voice down.**'

Guy scuttled back inside the narrowboat.

'OK,' said the woman, appraising Jayden and Aisha carefully. 'I'm Miss Fanque, but you can call me Leila. You passed Guy's test, so I think you might be able to help me, but you'd better come inside and I'll explain.' She glanced nervously up and down the towpath. 'We really shouldn't be discussing this out in the open. You never know who might be listening . . .'

3

AISHA

Aisha peered over to her block of flats and her kitchen window. She could just about make out her mum waving at them. Aisha waved back, knowing she and Jayden only had a short time to find out what was going on here before the Mums turned up. She grabbed his sleeve and together they stepped cautiously into the cabin of the *Narrow Escape*'s cabin. It was a lot bigger than it looked from the outside.

'It's like a Tardis!' Jayden said, as Guy darted to the back of the boat, just out of sight.

Aisha had no idea what a Tardis was, but this place was cool, if you liked stuff that made you go '*Huh?*' The walls were lined with maps that had pictures of mythical creatures like unicorns, phoenixes and dragons pinned up all over them. Strange objects rested in every nook and cranny. There were so many photos on the walls. Aisha studied one closely.

'Jayden, is that Cousin Chris?' she asked, pointing at a photo showing the smiling face of a kid resting against the side of the *Narrow Escape*.

Jayden walked over. 'Yeah! That's Chris when he was our age. This *must* be the floating classroom Mum was talking about! Ooh, I think that's Anubis, the Egyptian god,' he said, getting distracted by an ornament on the vintage dresser. 'And look up there, Aisha, above the door – it's the Green Man.'

'Green Man as in . . . an alien?' Aisha asked.

Jayden shook his head. 'No, Green Man as in the pagan spirit of the forest.'

'Impressive knowledge,' Leila said, smiling. 'Would you like some lemonade? It's the Fanques' secret family recipe.' She bustled off to the galley kitchen at the back of the boat.

Aisha spied Guy edging a little closer. At last she could get a good look at him now. He was about the size of a two-year-old, had pointy ears, and his leathery wings were tucked close to his gravelly grey body. *What exactly is going on here?*

Guy glared at Aisha as he settled into a giant armchair. On the wall behind him was a large painting of a broad-shouldered, solid man with a low, neatly shaped Afro and moustache. He was dressed in olde worlde clothes. It was one of those spooky portraits where the person's eyes seem to follow you around the room. The plaque underneath read **PABLO FANQUE** so Aisha guessed he must be related to Leila somehow.

'That is the world-famous and much-respected Pablo Fanque,' said Guy, noticing Aisha looking at the portrait. 'Circus owner and magic maker, he founded the Secret Beast Club in the 1800s. Don't stare too hard; Pablo won't like it, you know.'

Aisha raised her eyebrows. This place just got weirder by the minute.

Leila reappeared, carrying a tray on which was a big jug of lemonade and some glasses.

'Please accept my apologies on Guy Goyle's behalf, Aisha,' said Leila, pouring out four glasses of the fizzy, pale liquid. 'He needed to get your attention to test whether you could see him, and it sounds as though he decided to take your tablet in order to do that. Not ideal, but at least you have it back now, hey?'

Guy grunted as he grabbed a book and started reading, ignoring Aisha and Jayden.

Aisha folded her arms, feeling annoyed, while Jayden took a loud slurp of lemonade, breaking the awkward silence.

Aisha could feel her frustration growing. They were all dancing around the most obvious question:

'But what *is* he?' Aisha asked, pointing at Guy.

Jayden spat lemonade all over himself, almost choking at the same time.

Guy glared at Aisha. 'Your rudeness increases by the minute. Maybe my instincts are failing me in my stone age.'

'Easy,' Leila said to Guy. 'It's a lot for outsiders to take in.'

She turned to Aisha and Jayden. 'Guy is a gargoyle made of living stone,' she explained. 'He's lived with the Fanque family for generations, though don't ask me how many. Even Guy's a bit fuzzy on how old he is . . .'

Aisha wondered just how old you had to be to forget your own age.

'But things like living gargoyles only exist in books,' Jayden blurted out.

Leila laughed. 'The magical creatures you read about in books are most likely real – if you only open your eyes to the magic all around. You see, it is our job to protect the rare and precious spaces in our world – we call them **Bewilder Bubbles**. People with magic sight are rare, and so are the magical spaces that are dotted all over the world. Within these Bewilder Bubbles live all sorts of magical creatures.

'Most normal humans can't see the bubbles. If they happen to get near one, they just feel a strong desire to walk round it or take a different route. But those with magic sight can see them and can even cross the magical barrier to meet the creatures inside.'

'How many people have this magic sight?' asked Aisha, doubtful.

'Very few. Magic sight was a gift first given to humans in this country by the Green Man – the pagan spirit of the forest, as you correctly said, Jayden. Many years ago they helped to create these magical spaces. You, my dears, have some of that same magic running through your own veins.'

Aisha's mind was whirring. Surely this was just make-believe, like the stories Jayden was always reading in his books?

'I'm the head of the Secret Beast Club in the United Kingdom,' said Leila. 'It's my job to make sure that the magical creatures living among us are protected.'

'And I am second in command!' Guy reminded Leila. 'Bewilder Bubbles and the creatures living within them are as ancient as me.'

'If we have magic sight, how come we've never seen these Bewilder Bubbles before?' asked Aisha.

'How often do you actually go outside?' said the gargoyle with a smirk. 'Perhaps if you didn't spend so much time with your eyes glued to a screen, or your nose stuck in a book, you'd wake up and see that the real magic has been here all along.'

Aisha thought for a moment. 'Do you mean that there might be a . . . Bewilder Bubble near Hackney?' she asked, reaching for her tablet.

'Are you serious?' Jayden exclaimed. 'You're really going to turn your tablet on at a time like this?'

'It's what I've been trying to show you all morning. Look.' Aisha opened her tablet and pressed play on a video someone had posted online.

A very grainy, fuzzy picture appeared on the screen showing a creature that looked as though it could have been a small unicorn . . . if you squinted really hard.

The voice accompanying the video was excited: *'Whoa, whoa, whoa! I was out for my morning jog, and I seriously think I just saw a unicorn! Either that, or someone has stuck a horn on a big dog. No joke!'*

'The caption underneath says it was filmed in

Hackney,' Aisha said. 'It looks like the scrubland not far from here.'

Leila took the tablet from Aisha's hands. 'Oh, now this could mean trouble. Pablo alerted us to a disturbance in a Bewilder Bubble near here – a magical power surge erupted from that area early this morning, and I was worried that the bubble had been damaged somehow. It looks as though a small unicorn might have crossed over. A unicorn inside a Bewilder Bubble is relatively safe, but any human can see it once it's outside the protection of its bubble. This is why we need your help.'

'But what can *we* possibly do?' said Jayden.

'I hate to admit it,' said Leila, 'but my ability to communicate with magical creatures, even my ability to clearly see the bubbles, is fading in my old age, and Guy isn't – how can I say this politely? – always the most diplomatic member of the

Secret Beast Club. But you two could really help to make a difference. Guy and I have the knowledge, and it looks as though you two might have the raw talent. Together we could make a great team. We must get to the Bewilder Bubble right away and find out what is going on.'

'But we're the least outdoorsy or adventurous kids in the world!' Aisha burst into nervous laughter. 'Think about it – we've lived practically next door to a Bewilder Bubble all our lives and we never even noticed it was there. Trust me – we're not the ones you're looking for.'

Leila looked at her quizzically. 'Why are you so quick to dismiss your skills? You might surprise yourselves. And time is of the essence! We don't want SUUCS getting to the unicorns before we do.'

'Sucks?' Aisha asked in confusion.

'We're not the only ones to know about Bewilder Bubbles. A cruel organization called

the Seekers of Unusual and Unique Creatures Society, or SUUCS for short, also seeks them out. But, instead of protecting these magnificent creatures, they wish to capture, expose and study the secret beasts for their own selfish gain.'

Guy jumped off his chair and began pacing up and down the boat. 'If a member of SUUCS noticed the disturbance or saw that video clip, the unicorns could be in very real danger.'

Jayden shook his head. 'Listen, the whole idea of tracking down magical beasts is just impossible.'

'Impossible or *I'm possible*?' Leila shrugged. She stood in front of the portrait on the wall. 'You've been terribly quiet, Pablo. Do you have anything you'd like to add?'

Suddenly the portrait behind Guy began to rock from side to side. Jayden's eyes widened and Aisha gasped in surprise.

Leila sipped her lemonade and smiled. 'Oh, here we go. Great-Great-Grampy is still a real showman.'

Aisha couldn't take her eyes off the juddering portrait. Pablo had the same intense eyes as Leila, and Aisha was sure his bushy black moustache just twitched. It *did*! And now his dark tweed suit was beginning to lift itself from the portrait until Pablo literally floated out of the picture frame.

'**You called me, my dear?**' he enquired, hovering in front of Leila and twirling his moustache with a flourish.

Aisha was too stunned to speak. The portrait of Pablo was . . . a ghost?

4

JAYDEN

Jayden gripped Aisha's hand. Who could have predicted how this day would turn out? Only this morning, he had been certain that:

- ☠ He didn't believe in ghosts.
- ⚡ Magical creatures only existed in stories.
- 💕 Books were better than the outdoors.

This afternoon, Jayden had discovered:

☠ Ghosts and living gargoyles are definitely real.

☿ He lived near a Bewilder Bubble, which he had only just found out existed.

◎ Even books can't tell you everything.

Pablo Fanque's ghost whirled past Jayden, making the hairs on his arms stand on end.

'Hello, Great-Great-Grampy,' said Leila. 'Meet Jayden and Aisha. They have magic sight and I'm hoping they'll help me –'

'Ah, possible new recruits for the Secret Beast Club!' Pablo smiled, drifting over to Jayden and

Aisha. 'You will need to prove yourselves first, of course!'

'Ex-*cuse* me,' said Aisha, hand on hip. 'We don't need to prove ourselves to anyone, actually!'

Pablo gave an echoey chuckle. 'Quite right, quite right, but I hope you do understand that it is a great honour to be part of the Secret Beast Club. Here, let me show you . . .' He spread his arms out wide.

The walls around them began to flex and warp. In the blink of an eye, the inside of the narrowboat was filled with magical creatures. Jayden could hardly believe it. It was as though he and Aisha had fallen into an old film that was slightly grainy.

Is this in Pablo's memory? thought Jayden. *Or have we travelled back in time?*

'Duck!' he yelled suddenly, pulling Aisha down, as a phoenix soared over their heads. Then they quickly swerved out of the way of a dancing troupe of unicorns.

Pablo glided over to Jayden and Aisha, and gazed at the magical scene he'd created. *If ghosts could pop*, Jayden thought, *Pablo Fanque would burst with pride.*

'I was the *greatest* showman in Victorian Britain,' announced the ghost. 'People travelled from every corner of the world to see my shows. Kings and queens and fortune-seekers. But none of them *ever* knew that my circus act was a cover for protecting magical creatures from humans who meant them harm. I dedicated my life to protecting these marvellous creatures in the Wild Beyond.'

'He means the Bewilder Bubbles,' Leila explained.

'Yes, the Bewilder Bubbles, as you youngsters refer to them now. I suppose an old ghost like

me must endeavour to keep up with the times —
even if the Wild Beyond is a much more fitting
description. Perhaps you will soon see for
yourselves. Sadly, I can't move very far from
my frame, or I would be leading the charge.'

Aisha and Jayden gazed in awe at the amazing
scene before them, too stunned to speak.

'You have the magic sight, but it is still a
sacred honour to be asked to be part of this club,'
Pablo said, looking lovingly at the magical
creatures.

A lone unicorn trotted over to Aisha. Jayden
watched, transfixed, as the creature bowed its
head and gently nudged her arm. Before Jayden
could say anything, Aisha had already reached
out her hand to stroke the unicorn's glistening
white mane.

Jayden gasped.

A faint aurora surrounded Aisha and the

unicorn. It almost looked like they were communicating somehow . . . But that couldn't be possible, could it?

Quietly, the unicorn rejoined its troupe. When Jayden turned round, he noticed that Leila and Guy were also open-mouthed, gawking at Aisha.

'Why are you all staring at me?' said Aisha, frowning.

'Did the unicorn speak to you?' asked Pablo.

Aisha shrugged. 'Umm, yeah.'

'**Amazing!**' exclaimed Leila. '**What did it say? Tell us!**'

Aisha looked over at Jayden. 'Didn't you all hear the unicorn talking too?'

Jayden shook his head. This magic stuff just got *real*.

'Very interesting,' Pablo muttered, floating round in circles. 'Aisha can communicate with unicorns. Leila, you must take them to the Bewilder Bubble without delay!'

Leila grabbed Aisha's hands. '**You HAVE to join the Secret Beast Club, Aisha.** You can actually talk to unicorns! Do you have any idea how rare that is? You must

53

come with us – a disturbance like this is so unusual, and unicorns can be . . . hard to communicate with. **We NEED you!**'

Jayden took a few steps back as Guy, Pablo and Leila crowded round Aisha. He sighed quietly to himself. Jayden was happy for Aisha, of course. But he was the one who'd been learning about magical beasts since he was old enough to read. He couldn't help feeling a little disappointed that *he* couldn't speak to unicorns too.

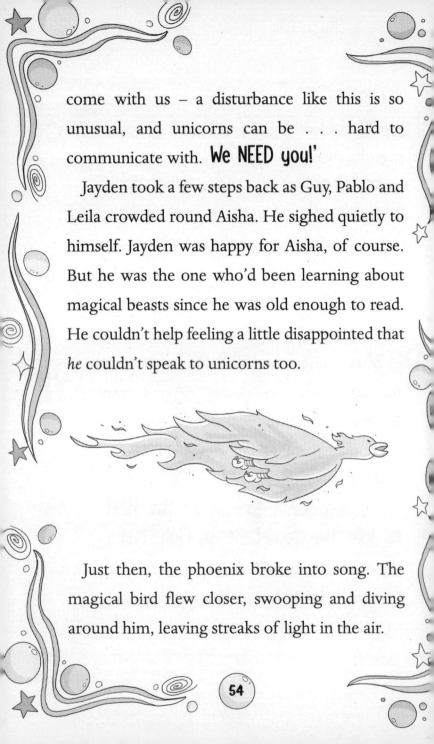

Just then, the phoenix broke into song. The magical bird flew closer, swooping and diving around him, leaving streaks of light in the air.

'It's so beautiful,' he whispered. Maybe just being close to amazing creatures like this was enough.

The phoenix, along with all the other magical creatures, suddenly disappeared. The narrowboat had returned to the way it had been before.

POP!   **POP!**

'**Oh no!**' cried Jayden and Aisha in unison.

Leila smiled at them, as though she could tell

Jayden and Aisha had fallen in love with the magical beasts.

'So,' said Leila, burying her hands in the big pockets of her trousers, 'are you up for the challenge? There'll be adventure and maybe even danger if you join the Secret Beast Club, but, most importantly, you'll be helping to take care of mystical creatures that need you. As humans destroy more and more of their peaceful habitat, they're finding it harder to stay hidden.'

Jayden looked at Aisha, and Aisha looked at Jayden. Then they shared a grin that could only mean one thing . . .

'YES!' they shouted.

Leila clapped her hands together. 'I knew Guy had picked the right kids!'

'Of course I did,' Guy said, looking smug. 'There is no better judge of character than a gargoyle; it's in our sediment.'

At that moment, a knock came on the narrowboat door.

'That's my cue,' said Pablo. 'Good luck, children. The unicorns must be protected at all costs!' And, with that, he floated back into his frame and transformed himself once more into a portrait on the wall.

Leila gave Guy a nod, and he quickly hobbled over to the corner where he froze like a statue.

A familiar jingle-jangle of bangles was coming from outside and hushed giggles that confirmed Jayden's suspicions.

'It's our mums,' said Jayden. *Curiosity must have got the better of them*, he thought.

'It's time for your first mission, kids,' said Leila.

'What is it?' asked Aisha.

'Convincing your mums to let you join my Nature Explorers' Club.'

'Hang on,' said Jayden. 'You mean, Secret Bea–'

Aisha nudged Jayden in the ribs and pressed her finger to her lips. 'It's our cover story.'

Jayden grinned and nodded.

Leila reached the door and, with one last look at everyone, she opened it with a big friendly smile on her face. After a whirl of bubbling hellos and introductions on deck, Leila showed the Mums into the narrowboat.

Their eyes darted around the small space. Jayden held his breath – what would they make of all the unusual things in Leila's boat?

He waited. And waited.

Can't they see any of it?!

Jayden looked at Aisha, who seemed to be thinking the same thing. Then she rolled her eyes and mouthed the words *magic sight*.

Of course, thought Jayden. *All these artefacts are magical.* The Mums didn't have the sight, which meant all they could see was an ordinary-looking narrowboat. They didn't even notice Guy; it was as if he was invisible to them.

The gargoyle gave Jayden and Aisha a sneaky wink. Aisha sniggered but quickly disguised it as a cough.

'Sorry if they've been causing you bother,' Jayden's mum said to Leila.

'We were getting worried about you two,'

Aisha's mum said, turning to Jayden and Aisha. 'We were putting some washing on the balcony when we noticed you two go inside the boat.'

'You mean you were spying on us,' said Aisha.

'Doing housework,' said Jayden's mum.

'*Your housework*,' added Aisha's mum. 'And you know better than to go on a stranger's –'

'You were right,' said Jayden, stepping in before Aisha could respond. 'Leila – I mean, Miss Fanque – does run a nature explorers' club.'

'I thought your boat looked familiar,' said Jayden's mum. 'Chris used to come to your club years ago. He still raves about it, even now.'

'Ah, dear Chris! He was one of my best recruits ever,' said Leila, pointing at the photo of him on the wall.

Jayden's mum squealed with excitement. 'I must message him and tell him I've met you. He'll –'

'Can we join the club, Mum?' Aisha blurted out impatiently.

'Please!' added Jayden.

'Goodness!' said Aisha's mum, taken aback. 'Miss Fanque, you must be a sorcerer to turn our two home-loving hermits into wannabe explorers. Normally we have to drag them outside for fresh air!'

'Oh, I can assure you there's no sorcery involved,' said Leila with a small smile.

'So, can we?' asked Jayden.

'We've already told Miss Fanque we would,' said Aisha.

The Mums shared a look. Jayden knew they liked to check everything out before agreeing to anything, so he wasn't surprised when his mum pulled out her phone. He moved a little closer to get a better look.

Chris, you'll never guess where I am.
Stood on the narrowboat with your
old explorer teacher, Miss Fanque.
J and A want to sign up. What do
you think? x

Jayden held his breath as the beep of a reply
came through.

DO IT!!! Tell J and A there's real
magic in nature if you know where
to look. And also tell them to
respect Leila's paintings! C ☺

Jayden's mum looked confused, but Jayden
knew exactly what Cousin Chris meant.

Meanwhile, Aisha's mum had launched herself

down memory lane. 'We were Girl Guides together when we were Aisha and Jayden's age,' she told Leila. 'We used to love going camping and earning our badges.'

'Those were the days . . .' said Jayden's mum with a wistful look.

'So, is it a "yes"?' asked Leila.

The Mums quizzed Leila on every possible aspect of the club, in what felt like the longest exam ever.

Leila might have steered away from any mention of secret magical beasts, but she remained honest about everything else. Jayden was impressed to see how she kept her cool under so much questioning.

Yes, she would look after them and, yes, she was an experienced explorer. Yes, there was a badge system so the kids could be rewarded for their involvement and, no, there wasn't any homework. Yes, it would involve lots of being outside and finding magic in the nature all around them. (Leila may have had a sneaky smile on her face when she said the word *magic* . . .) No, they didn't need a uniform. In fact, Leila was happy to lend them her binoculars (she passed a pair to Jayden) and a compass, which she shoved into Aisha's hands. Yes, they would get lots of exercise!

'Well,' said Aisha's mum, beaming with delight after they had finally run out of questions. 'This sounds just great. When can they start?'

'They can start right now, if you like?' said Leila. 'The first badge is for tracking.'

'Tracking, like animal tracking?' asked Aisha's mum, raising an eyebrow. 'I don't think you'll find much wildlife around here.'

'Oh, you'd be surprised,' said Leila, giving the kids a secret wink.

5
AISHA

Aisha looked calm on the outside, but on the inside her heart was racing. They'd done it! **They were now officially part of the Secret Beast Club!** In a few minutes she would be on her way with Jayden, a talking gargoyle and the owner of a magical boat to track down unicorns in Hackney. She'd never cared much about the patches of scrubland close to where she lived, but she suddenly had a desire to go there and protect it immediately. For the first time in her life, Aisha was actually looking forward to being outside.

After setting a world record for the longest 'goodbye and thank you and be home in time for tea' ever, the Mums were finally gone.

'Come on,' said Leila. 'We haven't a moment to lose.'

The foursome quickly made their way down the canal path, past the blocks of flats, across the traffic-clogged Marshgate Bridge and on to a smaller road that led towards the scrubland beyond. Aisha's attention was drawn to the road sign: Silver Street. Why had she never noticed

this road before? And why did she feel a tingle like . . . magic?

Eventually the sounds of people and the traffic fell away as they left Silver Street behind and ventured further into the scrubland.

'I'm not a fan of mud,' said Jayden, frowning.

Aisha pulled out her tablet and scrolled to the unicorn video. 'Look, this *must* have been taken near here. I can hear a narrowboat's horn in the background noise – listen.'

Before Jayden could protest about his trainers

getting dirty, Aisha grabbed his arm and followed Leila into the muddy marshland.

'Look,' said Leila, pointing at a snapped twig on a low-hanging tree. 'A creature passed by here.'

Aisha walked over, kicking her way through the weeds and moss, watching the ground as she went. She blinked and came to a stop. It couldn't be . . . could it?

'Err, I think I've found a . . . hoofprint?'

Leila rushed over to her and knelt down. 'These are unicorn tracks, which means a unicorn has strayed from its Bewilder Bubble. But where is it now?'

'There are more tracks over here,' called Guy.

'That doesn't make any sense,' said Leila, standing up. 'These prints go round in circles.'

'Maybe the unicorn was looking for something?' suggested Jayden.

'Yes,' said Leila thoughtfully. 'But what? What

would be so important that a unicorn would risk leaving the Bewilder Bubble for it?'

'Maybe they *all* left,' Aisha said, pointing at the ground. 'Look over here. There are too many hoofprints to be just one unicorn, aren't there?'

Leila's expression changed from confusion to concern. 'Oh dear. This is not good at all. See how deep these grooves are? I think these unicorns were galloping. I really hope no humans got in their way.'

'Aren't unicorns a bit too cute to be dangerous?' Aisha asked.

Jayden laughed and shook his head. 'Most people think that, but my book says that unicorns are powerful and can be vicious too.'

'Indeed,' said Leila. 'I saw the power of a unicorn herd when I was a little girl. I was so excited to see my first unicorn; it was my first Secret Beast Club adventure. We were invited to

celebrate the birth of a unicorn foal in the Highlands of Scotland, but it almost turned into a disaster when the force of the unicorns' celebrations ripped a hole in the Bewilder Bubble!'

'Why?' asked Jayden.

'Unicorns have extraordinarily long life cycles,' explained Leila. 'There's only one born every fifty years or so. All the unicorns gather together to welcome the new foal. The last time it happened it caused a major magical power surge, and the celebrations damaged the Bewilder Bubble. But everything was fine once the foal sealed up the gap.'

'The *baby* unicorn did it?' Aisha said.

'It makes sense,' said Jayden. 'I once read that unicorns are at their most powerful when they're young.'

Guy cleared his stony throat. 'I know it's rude

to ask a lady her age, but, Leila, are you in your *mid*-fifties?'

'Yes, I am,' said Leila. **'Why – of course! You're right! It's been fifty years. The power surge must have been caused by the unicorns celebrating the birth of a foal!'**

She stopped in her tracks.

'If there's a new foal, the unicorns might be edgy. Especially if the Bewilder Bubble has been damaged,' said Jayden.

'I think you're right, and this is where Aisha comes in. I've always had limited success at communicating with unicorns. The most I've ever achieved is a light nod of the head.'

'No pressure then,' said Aisha. She looked over at Jayden and half-jokingly rolled her eyes to try to lighten the mood, but he sighed and stuffed his hands in his pockets.

'You should be grateful you can talk to the

unicorns,' he said to Aisha, as Guy and Leila walked ahead. 'I've read *everything* there is to know about them, but I can't hear a word.'

A little sigh escaped Aisha's lips. It wasn't like Jayden to be snappy. 'I didn't mean –'

'Hey – check that out!' said Jayden.

'What?' Aisha said, glad that Jayden had been distracted.

'That slick car! Hang on a minute . . .' Jayden held the binoculars to his eyes and adjusted them for focus. **'Look at that!'**

He held them up for Aisha and she peered through. A shiny black jeep with black-tinted windows was driving along the road closest to the scrubland. Aisha could see a little silver unicorn ornament on the bonnet, and a small etching of a majestic unicorn on the driver's door. She watched the car as it sped away down the road leading to Wharf Row.

That made sense. A car like that had to belong to someone who lived in one of those huge, expensive houses there. Aisha had walked past the pillared entrance with her mum and Jayden the other day and they'd peered inside to see how the other half lived. It was full of mansions with sweeping drives and gardens backing on to a private section of the canal that flowed past the scrubland.

Perhaps we aren't the only ones looking for the unicorns? thought Aisha, and a cold shiver ran down her spine.

'Hey, look!' cried Jayden, pointing frantically up to the sky.

She followed his gaze and did a double take. The sky was shimmering and glittering above a patch of the woods up ahead.

'What *is* that?' asked Aisha.

Jayden gasped in awe. 'It looks like the Northern

Lights or something,' he said. 'But there's no way we'd see them here in London!'

Leila and Guy were a little way ahead, waving for Aisha and Jayden to catch up.

'I think this must be where the power surge came from,' said Leila excitedly.

The scrubland soon became denser as they moved into a smaller area of woodland. The Secret Beast Club used the lights in the sky to guide them and then suddenly Aisha saw a glimmering haze in front of them. It was the most beautiful thing she'd ever seen. **This must be the Bewilder Bubble!**

Aisha couldn't believe they had lived so close to it for all these years and had never come this way before. Stepping towards it, Aisha felt her heart lurch. There was a hole in the bubble. She could just about make out flitting, shadowy shapes moving around inside.

A deep, mournful, bellowing cry echoed through the gap. Aisha's stomach twisted in knots, a mixture of nerves and anticipation. It sounded like a horse and, because it was coming from inside the Bewilder Bubble, that could only mean one thing . . .

'Unicorns,' whispered Aisha.

She edged closer, but Leila pulled her back. 'Remember what Jayden said: unicorns aren't the sweet and cute creatures you might expect. We must be cautious.'

A rustling sound from the Bewilder Bubble grew louder, followed by the clip-clop of hooves. Jayden squeezed Aisha's hand.

Out of the spectacle of light came a fierce unicorn that towered over them all. It was much larger than Aisha had expected – a unicorn can make a horse look like a pony. Its nostrils were flared, and its warm breath blew down on them.

Jayden instinctively moved back, but something compelled Aisha to step forward. It felt like second nature to reach out and touch the unicorn's mane.

'WHERE'S MY FOAL?!' the unicorn bellowed with such force it knocked Aisha backwards.

'Is that why you're so angry?' Aisha asked the creature.

'Is *what* why it's angry?' asked Jayden.

'Oh, right,' said Aisha, remembering only she could hear the unicorn. 'It's looking for its foal. It must have got lost,' she explained to the others.

'**Not lost! STOLEN!**'

'Err, right, sorry, *stolen*. The foal has been stolen,' Aisha corrected herself.

The unicorn's breathing calmed as it lowered its gaze directly at Aisha. *'You understand me?'*

Aisha nodded. Though she was no expert at reading unicorn facial expressions, given this was the first day she'd ever met any, if she had to guess, Aisha would say the unicorn looked relieved.

'Follow me,' said the unicorn, and it turned to face the bubble.

Aisha took a step forward.

'**Whoa, where you are going?**' said Jayden, looking nervous.

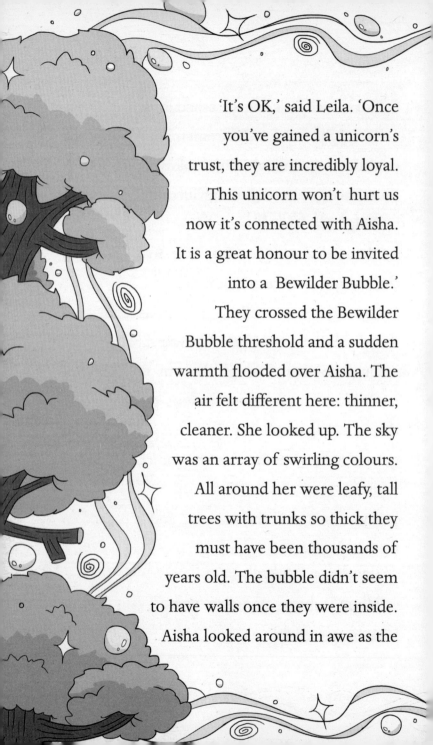

'It's OK,' said Leila. 'Once you've gained a unicorn's trust, they are incredibly loyal. This unicorn won't hurt us now it's connected with Aisha. It is a great honour to be invited into a Bewilder Bubble.'

They crossed the Bewilder Bubble threshold and a sudden warmth flooded over Aisha. The air felt different here: thinner, cleaner. She looked up. The sky was an array of swirling colours. All around her were leafy, tall trees with trunks so thick they must have been thousands of years old. The bubble didn't seem to have walls once they were inside. Aisha looked around in awe as the unicorn steadily led them deeper within the bubble until they reached a clearing where several more unicorns were waiting, all looking agitated and sad.

'How certain are you that *none* of the unicorns will hurt us?' whispered Jayden.

Aisha didn't have time to answer because the unicorn who'd led them into the bubble turned towards them and she could sense it wanted to speak to her. She gently stroked its side and was suddenly hit by a wave of fury and confusion.

'He's been *stolen*!'

'Slow down,' said Aisha. 'Tell me what happened.'

'My name is Stormsight, and my foal, Moonlight, has been taken. I am his mother. We were celebrating his birth, but the force of the surge from our celebrations took us all by surprise. It ripped a hole through the side of the Bewilder Bubble.'

'That's what we thought must have happened. But how did you lose the foal?' asked Aisha.

'**He wasn't lost! He was TAKEN!** We needed his magic to seal the hole again, but once we'd noticed the hole, he'd disappeared. We went looking for him, of course, guessing that he must have wandered through to the other side, but it was too late – Moonlight was gone! A human must have taken him. It's the only explanation. No creature in the animal kingdom would have harmed our foal. Only humans are capable of such treachery.'

'That's terrible!' said Aisha. She *never* usually cried, but she couldn't stop a tear trickling down her cheek. The magical connection to the unicorns was so strong that she *felt* their pain.

Leila touched Aisha's shoulder gently. 'Breathe, Aisha. And then you must tell us exactly what the unicorn said.'

'**The foal has been kidnapped!**' Aisha said, wiping her eyes.

Once Aisha had filled them in on what the unicorn had told her, Leila tutted.

'Hmmm, I think I know *exactly* who stole the foal!' Then Leila curtsied to the unicorns as a sign of respect before addressing them. 'I believe this to be an orchestrated attack by SUUCS. A jogger posted some grainy footage of your foal in the wood and someone from SUUCS must have travelled here to investigate. Seeing your foal outside the bubble, they took him, I believe.'

The group of unicorns pounded their hooves into the ground in rage.

Leila took a step forward, holding Stormsight's gaze. 'My name is Leila Fanque, and I am the great-great-granddaughter of Pablo Fanque.'

'*Is this true?*' one of the other unicorns asked Aisha.

'It is,' she replied. 'You've heard of him?'

'*Every magical beast has heard of the great Pablo Fanque.*'

'I am the head of the Secret Beast Club for this

land, and these are our new recruits,' Leila continued, with a confidence that Aisha found impressive. 'We're here to help. Please trust us.'

Stormsight nodded and turned to face Aisha. *'We have a deep respect for the Secret Beast Club and hold Pablo Fanque in high regard, but humans have become destructive. They care little for the environment or for sharing it peacefully with other creatures. I would have trampled on you all straight away if it wasn't for the fact that you could understand me.'*

Aisha gulped, feeling the pressure. 'Please, listen to Leila. She only wants to help keep you all safe and hidden from sight.'

The unicorn flared her nostrils. *'Now is not the time to hide! Humans have stolen my newborn foal. That means we are ready to GO TO WAR!'*

'What did she say?' Leila asked Aisha, looking worried.

'Ummm . . . well, they don't want to stay in the

Bewilder Bubble. They are ready to go to . . . war to find the foal themselves.'

'**No,**' pleaded Leila. '**I urge you to be cautious.** SUUCS will be expecting you to attack. They'll want to draw you out into the open; you'll be playing right into their hands –'

'*SILENCE!*' bellowed Stormsight, stamping her hoof so forcefully that no one needed to speak unicorn to understand what she meant.

The unicorn nudged Aisha. '*What do you say?*'

'I say, hear me out – I have a plan,' declared Aisha.

6

JAYDEN

Jayden had a bad feeling about this. Aisha had been his closest friend for a long time, and he knew that she always liked to act first and think later. Whenever Aisha *did* attempt to make a plan, it usually ended in one of three ways:

☺ Badly.

☻ Very badly.

☠ In a monumental, catastrophic disaster.

Edging closer to Aisha, Jayden attempted to do a mini sideways curtsey at the enormous angry unicorn standing next to Aisha, then whispered, 'I really hope you've got a good plan up your sleeve, Aisha, because right now I think we could be in *serious* trouble.'

'I know, Jayden. I'm thinking,' Aisha replied.

Jayden's mouth went dry. This was even worse than he'd feared. Aisha didn't even *have* a plan. She was just making it up as she went along!

'She needs to make the speech of her life,' Guy muttered through gritted teeth to Jayden and Leila.

Aisha cleared her throat. 'I've only known Leila for a few hours –'

Guy groaned.

'– and I would be the first to suggest: act first and think later. That's how I roll.'

Yep, thought Jayden with a nod.

'**BUT**,' continued Aisha, giving Guy and Jayden a glare, 'there's way too much at stake. If your foal has been taken by a member of SUUCS, they'll be watching out for you. And you are not safe outside this bubble.'

The unicorns flared their nostrils angrily.

Jayden watched as Stormsight leaned in towards Aisha and another pang of jealously rippled through him. Though he wished he understood what they were saying, he waited patiently. It didn't really matter whether he could talk to them or not – the main thing now was to keep them safe.

'I'm glad you asked,' said Aisha to the unicorns, 'because I know exactly what I think you should do.'

Uh-oh, Jayden thought. *The classic repeat-the-question-back tactic.* Aisha was always doing this to him and the Mums; it meant she was stalling for time.

The unicorns looked flustered and circled Aisha. Jayden could only see glimpses of his friend as the unicorns jostled for position.

'I totally understand that you're willing to do whatever it takes to get your foal back,' Aisha said, standing firm, her head held high. 'But you need a home to bring him back to. You don't know this world like we do. If you gallop out there now, you'll not only expose yourselves and the Bewilder Bubble, but you may lose your foal forever.'

The unicorns stopped circling and listened. Aisha's words had sunk in. Jayden smiled, feeling really proud of his friend. They were listening to her – *really* listening to her.

Aisha took a deep breath and rolled her shoulders back. 'Please, give us . . . twenty-four hours to rescue your foal. If we fail, then you can rampage all you like.'

Jayden gasped. *What was she saying?* How could they get the foal back by this time – five o'clock – tomorrow?! The baby unicorn could be anywhere!

Guy threw his pebbly arms up in despair.

'Give Aisha a chance,' Leila whispered. 'Earlier she didn't want to come on this mission at all, and now look at her! She has a herd of unicorns hanging on her every word. Twenty-four hours is better than nothing.'

The unicorns dispersed and Aisha rejoined Jayden, Leila and Guy.

'Great plan, Aisha,' grumbled Guy. 'Now that we're racing against the clock, where exactly do you suggest we start?'

'Umm . . .' She looked over at Jayden, her eyes silently pleading, *Help me!*

'Wharf Row,' Jayden said simply.

Everyone looked at him in surprise.

'*You* actually have a plan?' Guy asked.

'Better than that,' Jayden said, grinning. 'I have a lead. Remember that jeep, Aisha?'

Aisha nodded. **'The jeep – yes!'**

Jayden quickly filled in Leila and Guy about the jeep that he and Aisha had seen on their way to the Bewilder Bubble.

'It's got to be SUUCS, hasn't it?' Jayden suggested, looking at Leila. Maybe the foal was in the car when Jayden and Aisha saw it earlier. The thought made Jayden's tummy flip.

'A unicorn crest on the door and a silver unicorn ornament on the bonnet does sound like the flamboyant arrogance of SUUCS,' said Leila with a nod.

'Definitely suspicious,' agreed Guy. 'Jayden, I'm impressed.'

'I think we should go to Wharf Row and check it out,' Jayden said, feeling determined. But if they were going to go ahead with this mission, he had to do something first.

Taking a deep breath, he walked over to the unicorns. They paused as he approached, studying him hard. Jayden's heart beat faster in his chest. 'I know I can't understand what you are saying, but I just want you to know that we're going to do everything we can to rescue your foal.'

He bowed to the unicorns, and they bowed back. He looked over at Aisha, who was smiling, and a warm sense of pride ran through him. For the first time, he really felt like the unicorns were trusting him to help, and it was such a good feeling!

Jayden, Aisha, Leila and Guy made their way back to the hole in the Bewilder Bubble, accompanied by Stormsight.

Aisha stroked her mane. 'I won't let you down, I swear,' she said. 'On my life.'

Jayden's heart skipped a beat. *This was no fairy-tale adventure.*

· . ˙ ⁺ ˙ ⁺ ˙ ⁺ ˙ ⁺ ˙ . ·

It was already early evening by the time they had made their way through the boggy scrubland and back to the road that led to Wharf Row.

Leila led the way in. They walked along the road, looking for the black jeep.

Jayden gawped at the houses around him. Each home was bigger than the last and fit for royalty.

'I reckon every driveway is bigger than both our flats combined,' Jayden said to Aisha.

'Check that out,' whispered Aisha, pointing to a large house on the corner.

On the entrance porch of the mansion were two stone unicorns. And the jeep they had seen earlier was parked in the driveway.

'Look at those statues,' said Guy. 'Talk about making a statement.'

'Right,' said Leila. 'I'll handle this. Guy, you'd better stay out of view, just in case. Jayden and Aisha, come with me.'

They did as they were told, following Leila as she marched up to the massive double front door.

Jayden wasn't surprised to see that even the door knocker was shaped like a unicorn's hoof.

Whoever lived here was unicorn-*obsessed*. This *had* to be the place they were looking for.

Leila gave three firm knocks. No one answered, but Jayden could hear voices coming from inside. Leila knocked again, louder this time.

Eventually the door swung open. A tall man, wearing a deep-red velvet jacket with a unicorn crest on the breast pocket, stood in the doorway and glowered at them, as if they'd interrupted something very important. He had an official-looking folder, embossed with mini unicorns, tucked under one arm.

Jayden peered behind the man into the house. There were glass statues, also of unicorns, on either side of the galleried hallway and a crystal chandelier hung from the ceiling. Behind a large coffee table, he spotted a kid of about his age who was clearly hanging around to eavesdrop.

'Are you lost?' the man snapped, looking up

and down at Leila's mud-stained clothes.

Leila didn't let his rudeness put her off. She cleared her throat. '*I* am Leila Fanque, the head of the Secret Beast Club, and I have reason to suspect that *you* are harbouring a unicorn on these premises.'

Jayden watched as the colour drained from the man's face. His eyes opened so wide, and his head looked like it might explode at any minute. But, as quick as a change in the wind, the man recovered and began to laugh.

'Whoever heard of such a *ridiculous* notion! Unicorns aren't real. Now, if you will excuse me, I'm preparing for a very important dinner party this evening . . .'

The man attempted to shut the door, but Leila wedged it open with her foot.

Her eyes narrowed. 'I'm on to you,' she said.

The man's face went as deep red as his jacket.

'You are trespassing on private property. Now leave before I call the police!'

Leila held the man's gaze for a moment before stepping back and gesturing for Jayden and Aisha to join her. They turned to leave and, as they did so, Jayden heard the boy in the hallway say something:

'Dad, don't you think –?'

'Silence, Oscar! Remember family rule thirty-three: children are to be seen and not heard.'

The man slammed the door shut, but it was too late. Jayden had seen and heard enough to know everything he needed to know:

- ✵ The man's reaction to the Secret Beast Club meant that he *had* heard of it.

- ➡ It suggested he was a member of SUUCS.

- 💡 The way he was clutching that unicorn-covered folder showed that it contained something important.

- 🏠 The foal, Moonlight, must be somewhere in that house.

- 😁 The man was no match for the Secret Beast Club.

7

AISHA

Aisha felt like she was in a cop movie, staking out the house of a multi-millionaire unicorn-kidnapper. Except it wasn't a film; this was her real life! The four of them were crouched down behind a prickly hedge opposite the house, watching as glamorous guest after guest began to arrive, all in the most luxurious cars in the world.

One woman dressed in a glittering blue dress stepped out of a silver Tesla, and the diamonds on her necklace were so big that when they caught the glint of the porch light they momentarily dazzled Aisha's eyes. These people were clearly *LOADED* with a capital L.

Leila glanced at her watch and gasped. 'I'd better text your mums.'

She quickly tapped out a message:

> Hi there . . . we're tracking a creature and practising observation skills. Kids fine and having fun!

Ha! I guess that's true enough, thought Aisha as she peered over at the text.

Then her attention was grabbed by another car arriving. The gravel drive creaked and crunched as an Aston Martin pulled up. Two men in smart suits and shiny shoes rushed out of the car, chatting away *very* excitedly. Just as the front door of the house opened, Leila's phone beeped loudly.

Aisha held her breath as the rude man in the red velvet jacket scanned the road up and down. They all stayed stiller than a gargoyle.

'Phew,' said Jayden when the man closed the front door. 'I thought we were busted!'

Guy started grumbling about the first rule of a stake-out being *Silence your phone!* Aisha read the text from her mum over Leila's shoulder.

> Amazing! Glad they're having fun! Would be great if they could be home for dinner and bed soon. 😬 😴

Aisha rolled her eyes. The Mums were constantly trying to get her and Jayden to go outside, and now they finally *were* outside – and doing something very important – the Mums were worried about bedtime!

Before she could grumble to Jayden, a white Lamborghini rolled up to the house, with unicorns etched into the wheels. Aisha watched as a woman and two boys a few years younger than Aisha and Jayden stepped out. Just like the last two guests, they were all chatting very excitedly. Aisha strained to hear what they were saying, but she was too far away to make it out. This was no good! She ducked out from behind the bushes and, keeping low, she dashed across the road.

'Come back!' Jayden whispered.

But Aisha didn't turn back. Her gut was telling her this was her best chance to keep her promise to the unicorns. She crept closer to the front of the drive and crouched behind a unicorn-shaped hedge. From here, Aisha could just about make out what the boys were chattering about:

'. . . I can't wait for the big reveal!'

'Lucky Oscar, getting hold of a creature like that!'

They *had* to be talking about Moonlight! Aisha chanced a step closer towards the house. The front window on the right was the only one with lights on, but the curtains were drawn. It seemed like these were the final guests and, at last, the road was silent.

Aisha felt a hand on her shoulder and jumped.

'It's not safe to be this close,' said Leila. Jayden and Guy crept over to join her.

'But we have to do something,' said Aisha urgently. 'The foal is in there. I *know* it.'

Just then, the front door opened, and the velvet-jacketed man stepped out. He brandished a powerful torch and swept it up and down the road, shining it on the bushes right next to where they were hiding. The Secret Beast Club ducked down as low as they could.

'I agree with you, Aisha,' Leila whispered. 'But there's no way we are going to be able to just barge in there and take the unicorn with so many people around.'

'But we're running out of time!' Aisha pleaded.

Leila shook her head. 'There could be a dozen SUUCS members inside! And that man's on high alert. If we're going to break in and rescue the unicorn, it has to be when no one's expecting it,' she said carefully.

'Leila's right,' said Jayden, biting his lip. 'We can't go in without a *clear* plan. The stakes are too high this time, Aisha. For real.'

'Guy – you keep watch and alert us *immediately* if anything happens,' said Leila decisively.

'Right you are,' said Guy, giving Leila a salute. 'If a member of SUUCS spots me, I'll be sure to stay as still as a statue. A gargoyle won't look out of place on a street like this.'

With that, he shifted into a more comfortable position and then stood stock-still, his eyes fixed on the house.

'Kids, I promised your mums you would be home soon, so I'll have to take you back. But don't worry – I'm going to talk to Pablo and come up with a blistering plan to get that unicorn out of there before our time is up.'

Aisha let out a long, loud sigh. She could see she wasn't going to win this one, and deep down she knew that Jayden wouldn't be agreeing with Leila unless he was sure it was for the best. So, reluctantly, Aisha headed home with Leila and Jayden. She just hoped they were doing the right thing.

·⁺··✦·⁺✦⁺✦·⁺·⁺·

The Mums were waiting at Leila's barge when they arrived.

'Have you had fun?' asked Aisha's mum.

'Yeah,' Aisha and Jayden said in unison, sounding a bit deflated.

'They're just sad to come home, and they're tired from all the . . . nature,' Leila quickly explained. 'But I've promised the kids we can go out tracking again at the crack of dawn. We won't miss . . . a thing.' She winked at Jayden and Aisha.

They said their goodbyes to Leila and walked back to the flats.

'So, did you see anything interesting?' asked Jayden's mum.

Jayden shrugged. 'Oh, you know – this and that.'

'You both look shattered,' said his mum. 'I think a quick snack and straight to bed for you, Jayden. Right, see you two in the morn–'

'Ah, no!' Aisha and Jayden protested.

'Can't we have a sleepover at ours?' Aisha asked her mum.

'Please?' begged Jayden. 'We'll be meeting Leila first thing tomorrow morning anyway.'

Their mums looked at each other in silent discussion.

'Oh, all right,' Aisha's mum said. 'I can't believe you're so keen to go exploring outside again tomorrow!'

Aisha's mum made them some toast before ushering them off to get ready for bed. Aisha hadn't realized how achy she was after all the walking and creeping around today.

It felt good to be in her cosy bed. But sleep was out of the question. She could see the moon rising in the sky. It was half past nine, and the guests might even have finished dessert and be on to the 'big reveal' that the boy had talked about. Aisha couldn't get the helpless foal out of her head.

Stolen from his mother and treated like an object to be stared at. And what was in Mr Velvet-Jacket's folder? She felt sick thinking about what he might have in store for the foal.

Aisha tried to sleep, but it was hopeless. She lay awake for hours, just thinking. She could hear Jayden tossing and turning on the blow-up mattress on the floor next to her bed.

'Are you asleep?' whispered Aisha.

'Of course not,' Jayden whispered back. 'I can't stop thinking about the little unicorn, trapped in that horrible house. We've got less than –' he checked Aisha's alarm clock: 2 a.m. – '*fifteen* hours left to find the foal! The unicorns aren't going to wait a second longer than that before they leave the Bewilder Bubble and go on the rampage!'

All of a sudden, Aisha felt a fierce connection with the unicorn herd. It felt like a bolt of lightning hitting her chest. She leapt out of bed, ready for action with her hoodie already over her PJs and warm socks on her feet. She peered through a gap in her bedroom curtains. In the distance she could make out the bright, swirling lights above the scrubland where the Bewilder Bubble was hidden.

'Uh-oh.'

'*Uh-oh* – what?' said Jayden, sitting up.

'It's the unicorns. I can feel their frustration, and it just reached a whole new level. I think . . . I think some of them have broken their promise and left the Bewilder Bubble. It feels as though our time might already be up.'

'We have to do something!' Jayden said urgently.

Aisha looked gratefully at her friend.

'Jayden – *I'm* impressed!' she said. 'There's no way you would have broken the rules this time last week to sneak out at night and break into a house to rescue a unicorn!'

'Whoa, whoa, whoa,' said Jayden, holding his hands up. 'I just meant that we should go and tell Leila what's happened.'

Jayden pulled a jumper on over his pyjamas and slipped his feet into his trainers. 'It looks like you weren't going to wait till morning anyway, since you're already dressed!'

Aisha gave Jayden a mischievous grin and quickly wrote a note for her mum.

Hey Mum,

Left super early this morning for tracking. Took biscuits - animals love them.

Aisha x

'That should do – in case Mum wakes up and finds us gone,' whispered Aisha, showing Jayden the note.

'Now I'm impressed,' said Jayden, grinning. **'Good planning!'**

Aisha was secretly impressed with herself too. This was the sort of careful planning that Jayden usually handled, but check her out now – thinking ahead for once!

They crept out of the flat and down the flight of stairs to the main entrance. Careful not to make a sound, Aisha and Jayden pushed open the door and headed quickly outside. They had barely reached the canal path when they bumped straight into Leila.

'I was just coming to get you,' said Leila, sounding flustered. 'Pablo and I have been up all night thinking things through, and then he sensed it – the unicorns have broken their promise, haven't they? There are unicorns running around Hackney right now, looking for their foal. I hope I'm wrong, Aisha, but from the look on your face I have a terrible feeling that I am right.'

'I'm afraid so,' said Aisha.

'In that case, there isn't a moment to lose. Hackney is a vibrant place that never sleeps, and unicorns on the rampage are bound to be spotted unless we get to them first and persuade them to come back to their bubble. Plus, they're violent when they're angry – humans are in danger too!'

'Where should we look first?' asked Jayden.

Leila shook her head. 'I'll have to do this part alone. I need you two to head back to the mansion. You're going to get the foal out of there, *by any means possible*, while I track down these rebel unicorns. It's a huge risk, and one that I didn't want to take, but I fear we're all out of options.

Do you think you two are up to it? You've been pushed in at the deep end on this first mission.'

'We won't let you down,' said Aisha.

'We've come too far to back out now,' added Jayden.

With one last wave goodbye, Aisha and Jayden raced back towards the mansion as fast as they could.

⋅₊ ✦ ⋅₊✦₊⁺ ✦ ⁺₊ ⋅⋅

'What in the Stone Age are you two doing back here?' said Guy in disbelief. 'Where's Leila?'

'Some of the unicorns have left the bubble to go in search of the foal,' said Aisha urgently. 'Leila's tracking them down now, and we need to rescue the foal. This time we can't wait!'

'Without Leila?' Guy asked uncertainly.

'We have no choice,' said Jayden. 'The safe

return of their foal is the only thing that is going to stop the unicorns causing serious damage – and I don't think unicorns care too much about the difference between members of SUUCS and ordinary, innocent people. We need to return Moonlight to the herd, and hope that Leila can round up all the unicorns and bring them back too. It's our only chance to end things peacefully.'

'Then there's no time to lose,' said Guy. 'We need to save this foal before the unicorns start a war they cannot win.'

8

JAYDEN

Anyone who knew Jayden would have described him as:

- 😐 Bookish.
- 🏠 Indoorsy.
- 😟 A bit of a worrier who plays by the rules.

So no one could have imagined that Jayden

would be sneaking around in the middle of the night on such a risky mission. It was still hard for Jayden to believe it himself, even now, as he and Aisha approached the high wall round the house.

'We need to find a way in,' Aisha whispered.

The danger of the situation weighed down on Jayden's chest. His breathing quickened. His legs felt like jelly.

'What if we get caught?' Jayden blurted out suddenly. 'This is *breaking and entering*. It's not a good look, Aisha. *Trust me.*'

Aisha chewed the end of one of her braids. 'I know it's scary and serious, but we've run out of time and options. Maybe this is a kind of "act first and think later" kind of situation?'

Jayden took a deep breath. He knew that *act first and think later* was so Aisha, but maybe just this once it could be him too?

'*Ooooouch!*'

A cry came from somewhere over the other side of the garden wall.

'Was that a unicorn cry?' asked Jayden.

'Nope,' said Guy.

Then there was a squeaky bellow. **'*That was!*'** said Aisha.

Noticing that some of the bricks in the garden wall had been arranged in a mosaic pattern, Jayden ran his fingers over the outline of a unicorn. It jutted out to give a perfect foothold.

'Climb up,' Jayden said decisively. 'You can talk to the unicorn over the wall.'

Aisha began climbing, but the mosaic bricks didn't go up far enough.

'The wall is too high, and I still can't see over,' Aisha huffed, and she jumped down. 'I need a leg up.' She looked at Guy.

'Don't even think about it.'

'You are made of stone,' said Jayden.

'*Living* stone,' said Guy, 'and I'd like to keep it that way, thank you very much.'

'Please?' said Aisha.

After a few more moans, Guy reluctantly agreed. Aisha climbed on to his shoulders and then called for Jayden to join her. 'If you stand on my shoulders, you'll be able to see over the top.'

'Why don't you stand on my shoulders instead?' said Jayden. 'You're the unicorn whisperer!'

'Because I'm heavier than you,' said Aisha impatiently. **Just get on with it!**'

Swallowing his fear, Jayden climbed up on to Aisha's shoulders.

'**Watch it!**' Guy warned, as the trio swayed from side to side, trying to stay balanced.

Jayden could just about see over the top of the wall. He scanned the grounds. There were unicorns *everywhere*! Well, thankfully, not real ones. The garden was full of landscaped hedges

cut into the shape of the creatures, with a large stone unicorn water feature in the centre.

Jayden looked up at the house. A large crest was hanging over the double doors that led into the back of the mansion. It showed a unicorn rearing up on its back legs and it reminded Jayden of how the angry creatures had looked in the Bewilder Bubble. Seeing the crest gave Jayden a funny feeling in his stomach. It was almost as if this family had seen unicorns in defence mode before.

Jayden turned his attention back to the garden. A dark shadow caught his eye. As it moved closer, it came into focus under the light of the water feature.

'It's him!' Jayden whispered.

'Who?' Aisha grunted.

'Oscar, I'm guessing. He was the boy I saw inside the mansion when Leila was talking to

Mr Red Velvet. Wait . . .' said Jayden. 'Oscar has Moonlight!'

The boy was trying to feed the unicorn foal some kind of treat. Moonlight, though, was having none of it, nipping at him, bellowing in fury and cantering away.

'Please, I'm not trying to hurt you,' cried Oscar, reaching out desperately to hold on to the foal's mane.

I wouldn't do that if I were you, thought Jayden.

This time, Moonlight whipped round and headbutted Oscar in the chest before dashing to a corner of the garden.

'OOOOOOUUUUCCCH!' cried the boy, spinning round.

Jayden's heart froze. If Oscar raised his gaze just a little, he'd see them.

'How much longer?' grumbled Guy. 'I'm going to start crumbling soon.'

'**Stop complaining,**' hissed Aisha.

'*Shhhuuuush,*' said Jayden, but it was too late.

Oscar had spotted them. He stared at Jayden, his eyes wide in disbelief.

This is it, Jayden thought. *We're busted*.

But Moonlight hadn't finished yet. Jayden watched as the foal took up a new position. Moonlight kicked his hooves into the ground and then charged at Oscar.

Horn.

Down.

Without thinking, Jayden grabbed hold of the top of the wall and pulled himself up and over. He dived at Oscar, propelling them both out of the way of the foal just in time. He watched as Oscar tumbled upside down into a prickly unicorn-shaped hedge. But as Jayden attempted to pick himself up off the ground, he heard the sound of hooves stomping on the ground once more. He looked up to see Moonlight staring straight at him. The foal reared up on his hind legs, lowered his horn and charged.

Right. At. Jayden.

9

AISHA

'Aisha, help!'

Aisha's heart skipped a beat. She stretched up desperately, but the top of the wall was out of reach. Suddenly she heard a low, grumbling, buzzing noise like a broken motor. Aisha looked down. **'Guy! You can *fly*?!'**

The gargoyle was hovering beneath her, lifting Aisha higher into the air.

'Seriously? You never thought to tell us you could fly this whole time? Why didn't you do this in the first place?'

'Are you going to complain or go to help him?'
Guy said. 'It's not easy to fly when you're made
of stone. I can't stay up much longer.'

Guy carried her over the wall, where they
landed on the other side with an almighty thud.

'AISHA!'

Jayden was being chased round the garden by
the unicorn, while Oscar watched on helplessly,
having climbed to the top of the fountain. As
Jayden came hurtling past Aisha, she stood in the
path of the foal, raising her hand.

'*Moonlight! Stop!*' she yelled.

The unicorn skidded to a halt in front of Aisha.

The instant her hand touched his horn, a warm
glow spread over Aisha as she connected with the
baby unicorn. She felt his fear and anger but also
his curiosity about how she knew his name. Aisha
gently stroked his mane to calm him down.

'W-where did *she* c-come from?' Oscar

stammered as Jayden helped him down from the fountain.

'None of your business,' Aisha shot back. *Oscar can't have the magic sight if he hasn't seen Guy,* thought Aisha. *Good.*

She turned back to the unicorn, who was looking up at her nervously. 'Don't be scared,' she said. 'We're here to rescue you.'

The foal snuggled into Aisha and spoke quietly: '*I want my mum.*'

'She misses you too,' said Aisha.

'*You've seen her?*'

'Yes, she sent us to come to get you and take you home.'

'*I shouldn't have run off! I just wanted to see what was on the other side of the bubble. But then I got lost and I ended up coming out of the woods into a space with fewer trees and more noise and strange smells. I wandered around for a bit, and then a nasty human*' *grabbed me and pushed me into a cage!'*

Aisha could feel herself boiling with rage. How dare someone treat a precious unicorn this way?

'They brought me to this house, and more humans came and gawked and prodded at me. They tried to pull off my horn, saying I was just a dressed-up horse!'

Aisha couldn't bear it any longer. She turned to Oscar and glared.

'Shame on you!' she snapped. 'Unicorns don't exist for your entertainment!'

'I know,' said Oscar quietly.

'They are majestic, powerful – and slightly scary – creatures who deserve to live in peace.'

'I know,' repeated Oscar.

'Then *why* did you kidnap this poor baby unicorn and parade him around in front of your friends?'

'It wasn't my idea!' said Oscar. 'I tried to stop Dad, but he wouldn't listen. Then I heard his *real* plan and I knew I had to –'

'What plan?' asked Aisha, her eyes wide.

'He wants to use the baby unicorn as bait to lure out all the other unicorns and . . . capture them and then . . . sell their horns!'

'That's despicable!' yelled Aisha.

'I know. That's why I've been *trying* to set this foal free. But he won't let me get close enough to help him.'

'Oh, how convenient. You just *happened* to be

trying to set the foal free,' said Aisha, not trusting him at all.

Jayden put his hand on her arm. 'I think Oscar's telling the truth, Aisha.'

'I love unicorns,' continued Oscar, holding back tears. 'My family have believed that unicorns are real for generations. We're in a society called the Seekers of Unusual and Unique Creatures but we never knew they lived in our actual city!'

'But it doesn't matter how much you *love* them – you don't have the right to steal one,' Aisha replied, and tutted.

'I didn't think it would get so out of hand,' said Oscar, looking at the ground. 'I was just trying to impress my dad. To get him to be proud of me. Someone posted a video of a unicorn online and I knew it had to be real. I called Dad and he tracked it down and brought it back here. I've never seen him so excited. Then he called some of his horrible friends. I thought they just wanted to *see* the unicorn, but then I overheard them talking about other plans and . . . well, you know the rest.'

'He does seem genuine,' said Jayden to Aisha.

Hmm. Aisha looked fiercely at Oscar. She had to admit that he did look as though he was sorry. It was clearly his dad who was the problem.

Before she could say anything, a bright light shone in their direction, momentarily dazzling Aisha's eyes.

'Oscar? Is that you? What's going on down there?' came a stern voice.

Oscar was trembling. It was his dad and this time he was wearing a floor-length red velvet dressing gown. He. Looked. FURIOUS!

'Trespassers! Get off my land! This is private property and that is MY unicorn!'

'This is your moment,' Jayden whispered to Oscar. 'Stand up for yourself!'

131

'No, Dad,' said Oscar, his voice wavering but strong. 'You've got to let them take the unicorn home.'

'**Silence!**' said Oscar's dad. 'Remember family rule thirty-three: children are to be seen and not –'

'**No, *you* be quiet!**' yelled Oscar, flanked by Jayden, Aisha and the unicorn foal. 'I have something important to say.' His dad took a step back in shock. 'We've mistreated this poor unicorn and we *are* going to let him go.'

'**Not so fast,**' said Oscar's dad, lunging forward and grabbing the unicorn roughly by its horn. '**This unicorn is staying with me.**'

Aisha was frozen to the spot, overcome by the sense of fear she felt through her connection with the unicorn.

Jayden sprang into action.

'**Let go!**' he yelled, barging into Oscar's dad with all his might.

Surprised, the man lost his footing, releasing the unicorn's horn as he stumbled. He tripped over his long dressing gown and fell backwards into his own fountain with a splash.

Guy leapt on top of the fountain and blew a raspberry in the man's face, but Oscar's dad just looked straight through him.

'Oscar, come back!' he shouted.

'This way!' Oscar beckoned, and ran towards the garden wall, brushing aside some ivy to reveal a hidden door. 'Go!'

'There *was* a secret door here all along!' Aisha groaned as she ran through it, with Jayden and the unicorn at her heels. Guy managed to nip through the door seconds before Oscar slammed it shut behind them.

'You should watch who you make enemies with,' Oscar's dad shouted after them. 'I'm not the only member of SUUCS who is looking for unicorns. They can't stay hidden forever!'

10
JAYDEN

Jayden was absolutely buzzing as he sprinted down the road with Aisha, Guy and Moonlight. 'We've done it – we've actually done it! Well, step one, at least.'

UNICORN RESCUE TO-DO LIST:

- 💕 Save Moonlight - done!
- 🌀 Find rebel unicorns - in progress.
- 🏠 Return Moonlight before the rest of the herd go on a rampage round Hackney - no time to lose!

Guy led them back along Silver Street towards the scrubland. They *had* to stay close to the shadows if they were going to get back to the bubble without being seen. Then all of a sudden Moonlight stopped dead in his tracks.

'What is it?' asked Aisha.

Jayden could feel the ground vibrating. And then he heard the sound of powerful hooves pounding the ground behind him. He turned to see two majestic unicorns racing towards them. One of them was carrying something on its back. Could it be . . . ?

'Leila!' cried Jayden. **'She's riding a unicorn!'**

The unicorns came to a halt in front of the Secret Beast Club crew, and the riderless unicorn let out a giddy neigh of delight, bending down to nuzzle the foal.

Leila puffed out her cheeks. 'What a night! I found these two galloping down Hackney High

Street, just metres away from a nightclub packed full of people – can you believe it?! It was a close call! I promised that, if they came back with me, we'd get their foal, and then – **oh my goodness! Aisha! Jayden! You saved the foal! You really did it!**' she cried. Then turning to the unicorns she swiftly added: 'And I was never in any doubt, you understand.'

'**Ahem!**' Guy coughed.

'And you, Guy. Well done!' said Leila, beaming.

'Listen, I don't want to break up the party, but we've got to go,' said Jayden. 'The man who kidnapped the foal is on to us. We're not out of danger yet.'

Sure enough, as he peered down the dark street to the brightly lit one beyond, he could see the distinctive shiny black jeep with a silver unicorn on its bonnet. It was driving up the road, headlights on full beam. Aisha saw it too.

They broke into a run, ushering Moonlight onwards. The group dashed into the undergrowth, heading for the scrubland

'I'll go with the unicorns back to the Bewilder Bubble,' said Leila. 'You two kids get home.'

'You can't go without us!' said Aisha.

'Let them come,' said Guy. 'They can handle this.'

Leila paused, then nodded reluctantly. The large, riderless unicorn ran up alongside Aisha and Jayden.

'*Jump on!*' it said.

Aisha helped Jayden to swing up and then jumped up herself on to the unicorn's back. With Guy flying behind them, they galloped back to the Bewilder Bubble, with Moonlight scampering along between the large unicorns. Now *this* was the Secret Beast Club life!

They soon reached the Bewilder Bubble. The Secret Beast Club dismounted the unicorns and watched them gallop into the bubble.

'Wait!' called Aisha. She moved to follow them, but Leila held her back.

'You must let them go,' said Leila softly.

'But I didn't get to say goodbye,' Aisha said sadly.

Jayden felt disappointed that he didn't get the chance to say goodbye properly either. Would this be the last time they would ever see a unicorn?

Seconds later, his question was answered: *nope*! A large, fierce-looking unicorn appeared from the Bewilder Bubble and raised its hooves at them.

'**Uh-oh!**' cried Jayden, getting ready to run away.

'Don't worry, Jayden,' said Aisha. 'She isn't angry. She wants us to come inside.'

The Secret Beast Club tentatively stepped inside the bubble. Up close, Jayden recognized the unicorn as the foal's mother, Stormsight.

Aisha reached up and stroked her mane.

'It's OK,' said Aisha. 'I know what it's like to want to act first and think later. I'm just glad we got back here in time!'

Leila watched Aisha and Stormsight with a mixture of fascination and envy. Jayden felt the same, but he felt proud as well. He had always known Aisha was special, and now the unicorns knew it too.

'The unicorns are sorry they went back on our agreement,' Aisha told the others, 'and they've said they will never forget what we did for them. We've earned their trust.'

Stormsight looked at Aisha with amusement in her eyes, and Aisha blushed.

'What did she just say?' asked Jayden.

'Moonlight filled her in on the rescue,' she replied. 'She said we were reckless and put ourselves in danger tonight, and she's grateful we went to such lengths to save her baby. She said that sometimes a situation calls for caution and sometimes action. And Jayden and I showed great skill in both.'

'A-HEM,' grumbled Guy.

'You too, Guy,' said Aisha, laughing.

Stormsight turned to Jayden and nuzzled into him. Jayden laughed. Suddenly it was hard to imagine a unicorn ever having a temper at all.

'She wants you to know,' said Aisha, relaying the unicorn's words to Jayden, 'that you are . . . a most loyal friend. Even though you were afraid, you did what you thought was right. She said it takes real strength to stand up for not only your friends but also your enemies when they need help too.'

The unicorn bowed to Jayden in a clear sign of respect, and his heart swirled with pride.

Moonlight joined them and Aisha gave him a tight hug before the Secret Beast Club stepped back over the threshold of the bubble.

'Now you must fix the hole, little one! Quickly!' Leila said to Moonlight.

The baby unicorn tilted his head and used his horn to heal the Bewilder Bubble. With one last bow, the unicorns were once more hidden behind the shimmering veil – visible only to those with magic sight.

Jayden thought back to his books. Nothing he'd read could have prepared him for meeting magical creatures in the flesh. Being part of the Secret Beast Club had taught him more than just facts. Now he saw the importance of protecting not just these majestic creatures but also the natural habitat surrounding them.

'Ahh, the unicorns are safe and hidden again,' said Leila, hugging Jayden and Aisha.

'Yeah, but we know where to find them, if we ever want to visit,' said Aisha.

The sun was rising. 'We should head back,' said Leila, 'and have some well-deserved breakfast.'

Jayden and Aisha grinned. They didn't need to be asked twice.

As soon as they were back on the narrowboat, Pablo burst from his frame, anxious for news. **'Put me out of my misery and please tell me the herd are safe and that you caught the scoundrel who did this!'**

'It seems that the scoundrel responsible doesn't have magic sight, so the unicorns of Silver Street are safe,' said Leila, fussing over Jayden and Aisha so they were comfortable.

Leila brought out an array of pastries, and they scoffed them down. It was only now occurring to Jayden just how long it had been since they'd last had a proper meal, and how long they'd been awake! He just about restrained himself from licking his plate clean. He looked over at Aisha. She seemed lost in thought.

'Are you all right?' asked Jayden.

'Yeah,' she said, shrugging. 'I just . . . I miss the unicorns already, y'know?'

'I know what will cheer you up,' said Leila. 'I think you've earned your first Secret Beast Club badge. Don't you agree, Great-Great-Grampy?'

'**Indeed I do,**' Pablo said, beaming. '**I think you may be our most promising recruits ever. Saving a unicorn on your very first mission – very impressive!**'

Guy passed Leila an antique-looking mahogany box. It had delicate designs of all kinds of beasts carved into the lid and on its sides. Jayden held his breath as Leila gently opened the box and took out two hand-stitched badges. She gave one each to Aisha and Jayden.

Jayden rubbed his finger over the delicate fabric badge.

'"Unicorn Care",' he said, reading the words sewn on the front. Then he flipped it over to find that the back was even more spectacular, with a hologram of a beautiful and majestic unicorn.

'Even when we can't see them, the secret beasts are never really gone,' Leila told them. 'Not from here,' she said, patting her chest, over her heart. 'This hologram is a reminder that the unicorns can always call on you if they should ever need help in the future.'

'Cool!' said Jayden and Aisha in unison.

Guy let out a stony laugh. 'For two kids who

were against even stepping foot outside, I think you're going to make superb members of the Secret Beast Club.'

Jayden and Aisha looked at one another and grinned. What a mission! And now they were official members of the Secret Beast Club, with their first badge to prove it. They couldn't wait to earn their second! They'd had a taste of the magic outside – and they wanted more. What magical beast would need their help next time?

MAGICAL BEASTS I'D
LOVE TO MEET:

- Unicorns ✔
- Dragons
- Mer-people

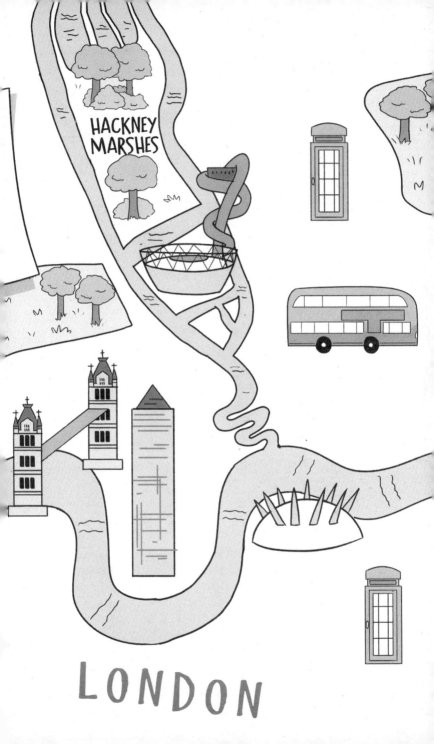

HACKNEY
MARSHES

LONDON

TURN THE PAGE
FOR SOME MAGICAL
EXTRAS AND MORE

SECRET BEAST CLUB FUN . . .

THINK YOU KNOW ABOUT UNICORNS?

Did you know that people have been writing about unicorns since ancient times? No one really knows where the myths came from, but many different ancient civilizations wrote about unicorns, including the Ancient Greeks, the Romans and the Mesopotamians.

In ancient Chinese mythology there is a creature called a qilin (or sometimes kirin), which is very similar to the unicorn, but is also part dragon and part lion!

 The word 'unicorn' comes from the Latin 'uni-', meaning 'one', and 'cornu', meaning 'horn'. So, their name literally means 'one horn'.

 People used to believe that if you drank from a unicorn's horn you'd be safe from all sorts of poisons, and that just a touch from a horn would purify water. It was even rumoured that Queen Elizabeth the First had a cup made from a unicorn's horn!

The unicorn is the national animal of Scotland, with two of these mythical creatures appearing on the Scottish coat of arms. Apparently, Scottish monarchs decided on the unicorn because it represented power and strength.

Unicorn foals are also called sparkles, and a herd of unicorns is sometimes called a blessing – that's how magical these amazing creatures are!

 If you want to dress up like a unicorn – or just eat lots of unicorn cupcakes! – then don't miss National Unicorn Day. It's celebrated in the United Kingdom every year on 9 April!

 And what about unicorn poo? Well, some people believe that they poo rainbows!

DO YOU HAVE WHAT IT TAKES TO JOIN THE

TAKE THIS QUIZ AND FIND OUT . . .

1 What three words best describe you?

    A. Brave, loyal, protective.

    B. Thoughtful, kind, creative.

    C. Funny, smart, quick-thinking.

2 What mythical creature would you most like to meet?

    A. A unicorn because they're so magical and beautiful.

    B. I don't mind – they are all amazing!

    C. A gargoyle – no other creature comes close!

3 If you were put in charge of a mission for the Secret Beast Club, what would you do first?

A. I'd get started straight away – there's no time to wait when a creature is in danger!

B. I'd do some research and make a clear plan of action – you can never be too prepared.

C. I'm not sure I'd want to be in charge . . . but I'd get stuck in with whatever I was asked to do by someone else (as long as the plan was a good one!).

4 What would you say if someone asked you about the Secret Beast Club?

   A. I'd change the subject quickly and distract them.

   B. I'd keep very quiet and pretend I hadn't heard them.

   C. I'd throw a tantrum and make a quick exit so that they'd forget all about the SBC!

5 What do you think the best thing about being in the Secret Beast Club would be?

   A. Keeping the creatures safe from harm.

   B. Getting to meet lots of amazing creatures.

   C. Going undercover.

MOSTLY As

Wow! You are definitely up for the challenge of joining the Secret Beast Club – welcome aboard! Just like Aisha, you're not afraid of getting stuck into an adventure or leading the way for others to follow. Your protective nature means you're ready to help keep any creature safe from harm, which is what the SBC is all about. But don't forget that sometimes it's OK to stop and think before you act, or you might get yourself into some sticky spots!

MOSTLY Bs

You're creative, clever and always one step ahead, which means you're the perfect fit for the Secret Beast Club. Like Jayden, rather than rushing in, you like to make sure that you know what's coming, and you're great at thinking carefully in a crisis, which can get you out of tight scrapes. You also love facts and stats, so you'll be able to work out how to approach the more dangerous creatures the SBC might come across. Just remember that you can't plan for everything, and taking a leap into the unknown can sometimes lead to the most exciting adventures . . .

MOSTLY Cs

You're a bit of a mystery . . . You love being part of the action but can vanish without a trace to keep everyone on their toes! Some people might think you're too much of a wild card to join the SBC, but – just like Guy Goyle – you're actually the perfect addition to any team. Deep down, you have a heart of gold, so you are definitely SBC material. Just don't always be so keen to head out on your own or think you know best – when you're on a mission it's all about teamwork!

Dear Reader,
Now that you've been introduced to the
Secret Beast Club, it seems only fitting
to introduce you to the team of writers
and creatives behind it. Robin Birch is the
collective pen name for children's writer
Rachael Davis and series creator Jasmine
Richards, who is the founder of Storymix
– the Inclusive Children's Fiction Studio.
Together with their editors, Clare
Whitston and Jane Griffiths, the Secret
Beast Club adventure took shape and
was brought to life by illustrator Jobe
Anderson, designer Jan Bielecki and text
designer Anita Mangan.

Since creating the Secret Beast Club
was such a team effort, and we've all
put a little bit of our hearts into the
project, it felt only right that Silver
Street made an appearance in this first

adventure, as this is where Jasmine grew up. Silver Street is in a place called Edmonton and is not very far from where Aisha and Jayden live in Hackney. When Jasmine approached Rachael about joining the team, Rachael was overjoyed because growing up she used to have many adventures with her best friend Alice, who lived in the flat next door, just like Aisha and Jayden. Rachael learned from a young age that magic is all around us, if we just know where to look . . .

We all hope you'll join us for more adventures with Aisha, Jayden, Leila, Guy and Pablo. Who knows what magical creatures they will meet next!

Robin Birch x

READ ON FOR A SNEAK PEEK OF THE NEXT

ADVENTURE . . .

Aisha and Jayden looked up to see her waving a piece of rolled-up parchment in one hand and a thick rope, which was glowing slightly, in the other.

Leila walked over to a small table and smoothed out the parchment. Aisha and Jayden joined her, curious to know what she'd found.

'It's a map!' said Jayden.

'Not just any old map,' said Leila proudly. 'This map shows –'

But before she could continue, a sharp **BBBBRRRRRRRIIIIINGG!** rang out from her phone.

'Oh, what a lovely surprise!' said Leila, looking at her screen and putting the caller on video-call mode.

The phone took a few seconds to connect before a thin elderly man of around eighty appeared on the screen. He was propped up in bed, wearing a hospital gown. He had a nasty bruise on his forehead and his left arm was in a sling.

'Goodness!' cried Leila. 'What mischief have you been getting up to this time, Frank?!'

'It wasn't my fault,' said Frank, shrugging his shoulders and then wincing in pain.

Leila raised her eyebrows at his reply and shook her head.

'I know it's been a while,' said Frank, 'but I need your urgent assistance. Something really BAD has happened and only the Secret Beast Club can help!'

Jayden was fairly confident about three things:

☺ Frank knew about the Secret Beast Club, so he must know that magical creatures exist too.

☺ Frank had had a recent mishap. (Possibly with a magical creature?)

☺ He and Aisha were about to embark on their second Secret Beast Club mission!

FIND OUT WHAT HAPPENS NEXT IN . . .

THE DRAGONS OF EMERALD YARD

COMING SOON!